CRIME AND PUZZLEMENT

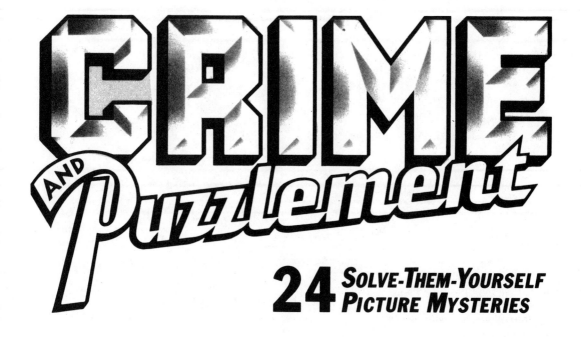

CRIME and Puzzlement

24 SOLVE-THEM-YOURSELF PICTURE MYSTERIES

Lawrence Treat

ILLUSTRATED BY LESLIE CABARGA

DAVID R. GODINE • PUBLISHER • BOSTON

First published in 1981 by
David R. Godine, *Publisher*
Post Office Box 450
Jaffrey, New Hampshire 03452
www.godine.com

Library of Congress Catalog Card No.: 81-47331

ISBN: 978-0-87923-405-8

Design and production by Hal Morgan, Inc.,
Cambridge, Massachusetts

Cover art by Leslie Cabarga

Thirteenth printing, 2016
Manufactured in the United States of America

CONTENTS

INTRODUCTION

Shortly after my nephew's eighth birthday, when he'd failed an arithmetic exam, hadn't made the team, had a hole in his pocket, and had lost his lunch money, and gotten on the wrong school bus, he came to me with a glint in his eye and all the excitement of Isaac Newton just after he'd been hit on the head with a Winesap and said, "You know what?"

I said, "What?" I'm quick on the uptake like that and the two of us spark each other off. *Con brio,* so to speak.

He said, "Look at this." I looked at one of the most miserable drawings that had ever come out of Miss Higgins's third-grade art class. She teaches it rather prettily, being pretty herself, but if she'd been a better teacher I would never have developed these puzzles, because I never would have had to ask my nephew what he was trying to draw.

In any case, I studied that hodgepodge of his and I pointed to one of the smudges, and I said, "What is it? A football?"

He beamed at me because I'd guessed wrong and he loves to know more than I do. "Does it look like a football?" he said.

It didn't and I said so, and he let me guess all over again. This time I came straight out with it. "It's a smear," I said.

He looked disappointed, but he was man enough to shrug it off and enlighten me. "It's a bullet," he said, "and it just killed a man and went right through him and that's why it doesn't look like a bullet any more."

I digested that before asking, "So who killed him?" I don't usually say the right thing, but this time I hit it on the nose.

"You!" he said, and burst out laughing.

That set me to thinking. If he could draw a bullet that had just killed a man and I couldn't even guess what it was, I could get back at him—which I did with my own drawing. It was no surprise to me that my nephew couldn't figure out what my sketch was supposed to show, and I admit that Miss Higgins wouldn't have been proud of it if I'd been in her class. Still,

I was intrigued with the chance of baffling my nephew. In fact, when he didn't say a word, I knew I was on to something.

I fooled around with my drawings for a while and showed them to a few friends, but I wasn't serious about the idea until I happened to show them to Wilbur Unisex.

Not many people know Wilbur. He has one of the finest intellects in the field of criminology, although that's merely a hobby of his. He's really a lepidopterist, and he goes chasing butterflies whenever he thinks he sees one. Unfortunately, he's a little nearsighted unless he's wearing his glasses, which he sometimes mislays, with the result that he's been known to invade girls' dormitories and police headquarters and even banks, always with his butterfly net and on the pretext of seeing a particularly fine specimen of *Utetheisa bella*. He shuns publicity, which is why his name isn't more familiar to the world at large.

When Wilbur realized that I intended to do a book of puzzles as a result of my skirmish with my nephew, he offered me his notebook and told me I could use any of the cases in it, along with the various outcomes. I grabbed the chance.

I've simplified the few that I've used, and none are so complicated that my nephew couldn't solve them, with a little help from Wilbur. Incidentally, Wilbur taught me a lot. For instance, he pointed out that criminology is not an exact science, and so the cases in this book deal with probabilities rather than certainties, which is the way the police work.

Neither my nephew nor I have drawn any of the sketches. They were made by the talented Leslie Cabarga, whose artwork has brought these stories into such vivid reality.

The various cases took place over a long period of time. Taking them question by question will usually guide you to the correct solution, but if you feel you're on Wilbur's level of a super-sleuth, skip the questions and head straight for the main answer. In either case, go to it and have fun.

CRIME AND PUZZLEMENT

HOW TO SOLVE THE PUZZLES

1. Always read the narrative first. It supplies you with vital clues.

2. Read all the questions through without trying to answer them. This will give you a sense of what to look for in the picture.

3. Examine the picture.

4. Grab your pencil.

5. Answer the questions, one at a time and in order. If you're a beginner, it might help if you check your answers as you go along to make sure that you're on the right track. Once you think your detecting skills are sharp enough, you may want to skip the preliminary questions altogether and go straight for the big one at the end.

6. Look at the solution and either congratulate yourself on a job well done or resolve to do better next time. Then move on to the next puzzle.

BOUDOIR

Amy LaTour's body was found in her bedroom last night, as shown, with her pet canary strangled in its cage. Henry Willy and Joe Wonty, her boyfriends; Louis Spanker, a burglar known to have been in the vicinity; and Celeste, her maid, were questioned by the police.

Wilbur Unisex, who happened to be in the area pursuing the *Heliconius charitonius,* put down his butterfly net and solved the case. Can you?

Questions

1. How was Amy apparently killed?
   Shot_____ Stabbed_____
   Strangled_____ Beaten_____

2. Is there evidence of a violent struggle? Yes_____ No_____

3. Was her murderer strong?
   Yes_____ No_____

4. Was Amy fond of jewelry?
   Yes_____ No_____

5. Was she robbed? Yes_____ No_____

6. Do you think she had been on friendly terms with her killer?
   Yes_____ No_____

7. Was the canary strangled before Amy's death? Yes_____ No_____

8. Was this a crime of passion?
   Yes_____ No_____

9. Did Willy have a motive?
   Yes_____ No_____

10. Who killed Amy? Henry Willy_____
    Joe Wonty_____ Louis Spanker_____
    Celeste_____

Solution on page 51

FRAGMENT

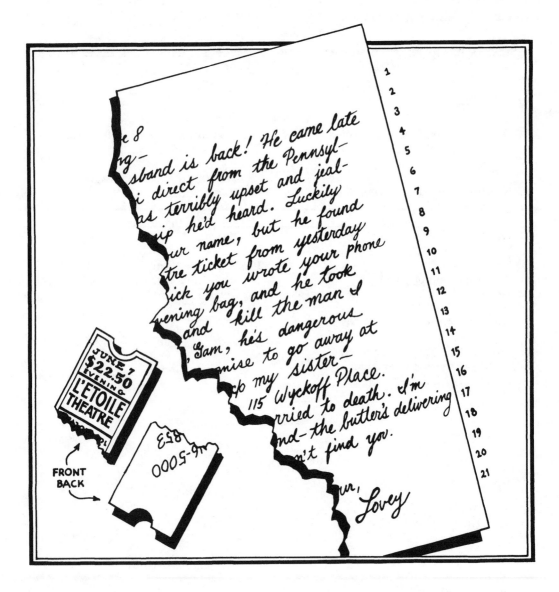

Gamut Ordway's body, pierced by two bullets, was discovered in a New York hotel suite, which he had rented for a few days and for reasons unknown. The torn halves of a theater ticket and of a letter, shown here, were clutched tightly in his lifeless hand.

From the two fragments, can you guess who killed him and why?

Questions

1. Was the letter written to Ordway?
   Yes_____ No_____

2. Was Lovey's husband in town? Yes_____ No_____

3. Was he dangerously jealous?
   Yes_____ No_____

4. Did he have the means to locate Ordway? Yes_____ No_____

5. Did Lovey take precautions against her husband discovering her affair with Ordway? Yes_____ No_____

6. Is the theater stub the one that is referred to in the letter?
   Yes_____ No_____

7. Reconstruct the letter as well as you can, completing as many of the partial words as you can.

8. Do you think that Lovey's husband killed Ordway? Yes_____ No_____

Solution on page 51

END OF A VILLAIN

Romano Rubitch was undoubtedly the most hated man in Endicott County, and his life was often threatened, even by children. Consequently, when his boat was found drifting in Dead Man's Cove without him, there was the equivalent of dancing in the streets. The widows and orphans whose life savings he'd invested and lost, the friends he'd double-crossed, the tradesmen he'd cheated, and the women he'd dishonored were of one mind: good riddance to bad Rubitch. And whether he'd drowned accidentally or been knocked off by a public benefactor, or had finally repaid his debt to the community by committing suicide was immaterial to most people. But the sheriff of Endicott County had a sworn duty to investigate, and he carried it out capably.

All he knew was that Rubitch had left his house on the morning of May 17 and had not returned for dinner, and that the next day his boat had been found exactly as you see it. If you were the sheriff, what conclusions would you draw?

Questions

1. Do you think Rubitch had been fishing? Yes_____ No_____

2. Is there evidence of a fight? Yes_____ No_____

3. Do you think Rubitch committed suicide? Yes_____ No_____

4. Is this a tippy boat? Yes_____ No_____

5. Do you think Rubitch fell overboard accidentally and drowned? Yes_____ No_____

6. Do you think the gas line was deliberately cut? Yes_____ No_____

7. Is the presence of the paint can unusual? Yes_____ No_____

8. Do you think that evidence of a fight was planted? Yes_____ No_____

9. How many people can you prove to have been in the boat? One_____ Two_____ Three_____ More than three_____

10. What do you think happened?

Solution on page 52

MERRILL'S ALIBI

Just as it started to rain at 7:00 on a November evening, Ferris Allen was shot and killed at his home by a rifle bullet that penetrated his left eyeball. His assailant escaped by outrunning the Allen watchman and scaling a high wall. Since the police knew that C. B. Merrill and Allen's gorgeous wife Euphrosyne were having an affair, and that Allen had threatened Merrill with dire harm, Merrill was an obvious suspect. The police therefore rushed to his apartment, which they reached at 7:40. He answered the doorbell and they walked into his living room, which you see exactly as it was when they entered. Merrill admitted that he could have reached the Allen estate in a half hour by car, but insisted that he had not.

"Euphrosyne was here this afternoon," he told the police, "and after she left a package was delivered. Around 6:15 I went out to buy a bulb, since one of mine had broken. Later on it started to rain, and I went out again around 7:15 to buy a paper. I sat down in the chair by my bookcase and was reading it when you people came in."

Euphrosyne said, through her tears, "C. B. and I spent an innocent afternoon reading poetry. He didn't go out until 6:45, when he bought a paper and a bulb and sent me home in a taxi."

Would you charge Merrill with homicide?

Questions

1. Could Merrill have outrun the watchman and scaled a high wall?
Yes _____ No _____

2. Is it likely that he was a good marksman? Yes _____ No _____

3. Is the fact that none of the guns in the rack had been fired recently evidence of Merrill's innocence?
Yes _____ No _____

4. If Euphrosyne's story is completely true, does it clear Merrill?
Yes _____ No _____

5. Had Merrill and his lady love previously agreed on their stories?
Yes _____ No _____

6. Do you think that she was in his apartment during the afternoon?
Yes _____ No _____

7. Can you prove that any part of Euphrosyne's story is false?
Yes _____ No _____

8. Had Merrill been out recently?
Yes _____ No _____

9. Check the assertions in Merrill's alibi that you can prove false: Euphrosyne was here this afternoon. _____ One of my bulbs was broken and I got a new one. _____ I was out after it started to rain. _____ I bought a paper. _____ I was reading it when you people (the police) came in. _____

10. Would you charge Merrill with homicide? Yes _____ No _____

Solution on page 53

A Matter of Diamonds

Mrs. Diana Dogge, Dr. C. D. Spaniel and Owen Weimaraner were having tea on the Dogge patio and examining some diamonds that Mr. Weimaraner was showing in the hope of selling. The diamonds were on the small, dark platter near the center of the table when someone inside the house yelled "Fire!" and the three fled the patio. The fire, which had been set, damaged a curtain but was easily extinguished, and it was not determined who had given the alarm. When the trio returned, the diamonds were gone.

Wilbur Unisex, who had been chasing butterflies, came upon the scene as shown. He questioned the trio and all of them gave similar answers to the effect that at the alarm they had jumped up and run into the house and that no one had noticed what the others did.

From a study of the scene, Wilbur guessed who had stolen the diamonds. And he was right, of course. He always is.

Questions

1. Where did Mrs. Dogge sit? A____
   B____ C____

2. Where did the doctor sit? A____
   B____ C____

3. Was the doctor nervous?
   Yes____ No____

4. Do you think the diamonds blew
   away? Yes____ No____

5. Does Mrs. Dogge's wealth eliminate
   her as a suspect? Yes____ No____

6. Had all three people left the table
   after making similar movements?
   Yes____ No____

7. Who stole the diamonds?

Solution on page 54

THE VAN BLIVEN NECKLACE

Mrs. Horatio Van Bliven loved caviar and bubble baths, and indulged herself accordingly. Part of her hotel room is shown, both before and after the disappearance of her $25,000.00 necklace. She said she'd locked her door and taken her bubble bath at seven o'clock, and she denied that the phone had rung, although the operator stated that it had.

The police searched three suspects and their belongings, and found nothing. The suspects were: Mrs. Van Bliven; Emmy, the pert little chambermaid; and Honoré Schmidt, who had an adjacent room which shared Mrs. Van Bliven's balcony.

Whom would you arrest for the theft, and what do you think happened to the necklace?

Questions

1. Which picture shows the room before the theft? A ____ B ____

2. Was Mrs. Van Bliven traveling? Yes ____ No ____

3. What three objects were apparently searched?

4. Is Mrs. Van Bliven's denial of the phone call incriminating? Yes ____ No ____

5. Was the pane of glass broken from the outside? Yes ____ No ____

6. Could Schmidt have entered via the French doors? Yes ____ No ____

7. Would Emmy's presence in the room have been incriminating? Yes ____ No ____

8. Is there evidence that Emmy was in the room? Yes ____ No ____

9. Do you think that Emmy broke the pane of glass? Yes ____ No ____

10. Is it possible that Mrs. Van Bliven faked the theft for the insurance money? Yes ____ No ____

11. Where would you look for the necklace?

12. Who stole the necklace? Mrs. Van Bliven ____ Emmy ____ Schmidt ____

Solution on page 54

DEAD MAN'S CURVATURE

The badly burnt body of Dicky Philander was found in the wreckage of his car at the bottom of a cliff, the top of which is shown. The exact cause of death was not ascertained for some time.

The insurance company, with whom Dicky had a $300,000.00 policy in favor of his wife, said, "Anybody who comes down that hill and goes right through the fence without even trying to make the turn is committing suicide, and our policy specifies that we don't pay for suicide."

His wife, Ellie Mosinary (she had kept her own name because she liked it so much), said, "Dicky had an assignation with Ronda Ravish at the Knocking Knee Inn, and he'd never have committed suicide when he had her ahead of him. This was an accident."

Ronda's husband, Daniel V. Ravish, said, "Ellie's right. Just an accident. What else?" What do you think?

Questions

1. Did Dicky's car go over the cliff at this point? Yes____ No____

2. Did Ellie have a motive for killing Dicky? Yes____ No____

3. Did Daniel V. have a motive for killing Dicky? Yes____ No____

4. Do you think that Ellie and Daniel V. knew each other? Yes____ No____

5. Did Dicky's car crash through the fence? Yes____ No____

6. Did Dicky's car stop before going over the cliff? Yes____ No____

7. Do you think that Dicky was killed before the car went through the fence? Yes____ No____

8. Do you think that more than one person was involved in the wreck? Yes____ No____

9. What do you think happened?
Dicky died in an accident.____
Dicky committed suicide.____
Ellie killed Dicky.____
Daniel V. killed Dicky.____
Ellie and Daniel V. conspired to kill Dicky. ____

Solution on page 55

Tragedy in the Bathroom

Minnie Verbermockle called the doctor and said, "My husband had a fall and he's lying unconscious on the bathroom floor. I think he must have been taking a shower and slipped on a cake of soap. I did not move him. I threw a blanket over him and called you immediately."

When the doctor arrived, he saw the scene as depicted and pronounced Horace Verbermockle dead as the result of a fracture at the rear of his skull. Can you tell what happened?

Questions

1. Were the Verbermockles compatible? Yes____ No____

2. Had Horace finished brushing his teeth? Yes____ No____

3. Had the shower been running? Yes____ No____

4. Had Horace just taken a shower? Yes____ No____

5. Had Minnie been in the shower? Yes____ No____

6. Did Horace slip on the soap? Yes____ No____

7. Had the soap fallen out of the soap holder? Yes____ No____

8. Did the soap puddle come from either the dripping shower or the washstand? Yes____ No____

9. Had the bottle been knocked over before Horace allegedly fell? Yes____ No____

10. Is there a possible murder weapon in the bathroom? Yes____ No____

11. Has evidence been planted to give a false impression of what happened? Yes____ No____

12. On the basis of the evidence you have developed, reconstruct what happened.

Solution on page 56

CHECK IT

$\mathbf{A}$ month after Louis Armand told his sons that each of them would inherit $200,000.00 (Hemini as insurance beneficiary, Gemini by will), Louis was found stabbed to death and sitting at his desk, on which Inspector Egmont found the articles shown. Both sons admitted having seen their father that afternoon, but each claimed to have left him alive and kicking.

Can you tell who killed Louis Armand?

Questions

1. Do you think that Louis intended to disinherit his sons? Yes_____ No_____

2. Did Hemini have a motive for killing his father? Yes_____ No_____

3. Did Gemini? Yes_____ No_____

4. Was payment made by the bank on both checks? Yes_____ No_____

5. Are the signatures of the two checks identical? Yes_____ No_____

6. Was one of the checks forged? Yes, the $5000.00 check_____ Yes, the $50.00 check_____ No_____

7. Who do you think saw Louis last? Hemini_____ Gemini_____

8. Who do you think killed Louis? Hemini_____ Gemini_____

Solution on page 57

THE LUNCHROOM MURDER

On an otherwise uneventful Thursday, police heard a shot in Ernie's Lunchroom, rushed inside, and found this scene.

They identified the body as that of Five-Fingered Fannin, a racketeer. Ernie, who had no helper, had only one fact to tell: The murderer had leaned against the wall while firing at point-blank range. The imprint of his hand is in clear view.

From these facts and an examination of the scene, can you answer the questions and tell who killed Fannin?

Questions

1. Had Ernie been mopping up recently? Yes____ No____

2. How many customers had recently been in the restaurant? None____ One____ Two____ Three____ Four____ Five____

3. Do you think Ernie was the victim of a holdup? Yes____ No____

4. Do you think B, C, and D knew each other? Yes____ No____

5. Did A enter the restaurant before D? Yes____ No____

6. At least how many people were in the restaurant the instant that Fannin entered? One____ Two____ Three____ Four____ Five____ Six____

7. Would footsteps show if they had not traversed the wet spaces? Yes____ No____

8. Which are Ernie's footsteps? X____ Y____ Z____

9. Did Ernie walk out through the kitchen door? Yes____ No____

10. Did Ernie ring up the $8.75 sale on the cash register before the murder? Yes____ No____

11. Where was Ernie at the moment of the shooting? Near the mop____ Near the cash register____ Near the kitchen____

12. Which are A's footsteps? X____ Y____ Z____

13. Did A run out through the kitchen door? Yes____ No____

14. Are the footsteps marked X those of the murderer? Yes____ No____

15. Did the murderer fire with his right hand? Yes____ No____

16. Who killed Fannin? A____ B____ C____ D____ Ernie____

Solution on page 57

EXTORTION

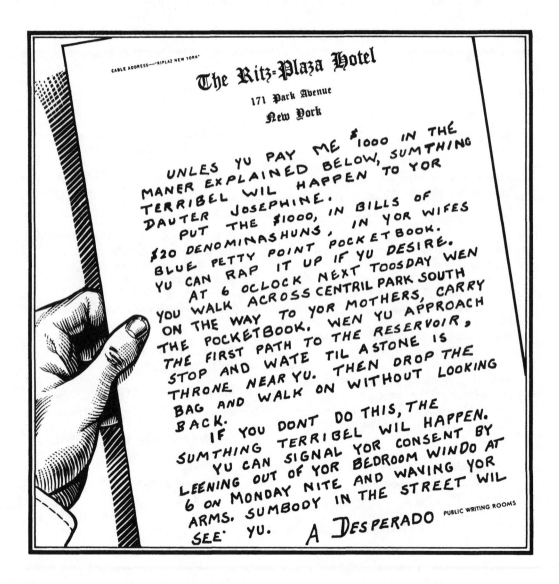

CABLE ADDRESS—"RIPLAZ NEW YORK"

The Ritz-Plaza Hotel

171 Park Avenue

New York

UNLES YU PAY ME $1000 IN THE MANER EXPLAINED BELOW, SUMTHING TERRIBEL WIL HAPPEN TO YOR DAUTER JOSEPHINE.

PUT THE $1000, IN BILLS OF $20 DENOMINASHUNS, IN YOR WIFES BLUE PETTY POINT POCKETBOOK. YU CAN RAP IT UP IF YU DESIRE.

AT 6 OCLOCK NEXT TOOSDAY WEN YOU WALK ACROSS CENTRIL PARK SOUTH ON THE WAY TO YOR MOTHERS, CARRY THE POCKETBOOK. WEN YU APPROACH THE FIRST PATH TO THE RESERVOIR, STOP AND WATE TIL A STONE IS THROWN NEAR YU. THEN DROP THE BAG AND WALK ON WITHOUT LOOKING BACK.

IF YOU DONT DO THIS, THE SUMTHING TERRIBEL WIL HAPPEN.

YU CAN SIGNAL YOR CONSENT BY LEENING OUT OF YOR BEDROOM WINDO AT 6 ON MONDAY NITE AND WAVING YOR ARMS. SUMBODY IN THE STREET WIL SEE YU.

A DESPERADO

PUBLIC WRITING ROOMS

Pictured here is a kidnapping threat which was mailed to Iver Nutmeg, wealthy gumshoe manufacturer.

From this information and an examination of the paper, can you discover who sent the extortion letter?

Questions

1. Did the writer know Nutmeg's address? Yes_____ No_____

2. Did the writer misspell because he was unfamiliar with English? Yes_____ No_____

3. Do you think the writer misspelled intentionally? Yes_____ No_____

4. Do you think the writer used print as a disguise to his handwriting? Yes_____ No_____

5. Would you say the writer was probably a shabbily dressed person? Yes_____ No_____

6. Do you think the writer was a professional gangster? Yes_____ No_____

7. Did the writer know Nutmeg by sight? Yes_____ No_____

8. Was the writer familiar with Nutmeg's habits? Yes_____ No_____

9. Was the writer familiar with Nutmeg's apartment? Yes_____ No_____

10. Do you think the writer was a man? Yes_____ No_____

11. Who wrote the extortion letter? A gangster_____ An elevator boy_____ A discharged English governess_____ A discharged office clerk_____ A waitress from the restaurant where Nutmeg eats lunch_____ A discharged Irish chambermaid_____ A discharged chauffeur_____ A delivery boy_____

Solution on page 58

Music Hath Charms

Oscar Toscanelli, clarinetist, Wolfgang Brahman, violinist, and his wife Cosima Brahman, pianist, performed together as The Classical Trio. They had been practicing all afternoon at the Brahman home, and around five o'clock Cosima went to the corner delicatessen for a loaf of salami, which they all favored. When she returned, she saw the room as sketched here, with Oscar and Wolfgang both dead of gunshot wounds, and Wolfgang stretched out under her piano. The gun is not shown.

Interrogated at the hospital where she'd been taken for treatment of shock, Cosima said, "I don't think they liked each other." After which statement she lapsed into a state of confusion, and was unquestionable.

Can you decide what went on between Wolfgang and Oscar?

Questions

1. Was Wolfgang a practical joker?
   Yes____ No____

2. Whose coat is hanging on the rack?
   Wolfgang's____ Oscar's____

3. Was Oscar a wine lover?
   Yes____ No____

4. Is Chateau Lafite an expensive wine?
   Yes____ No____

5. Do you think that Oscar had reason to be angry? Yes____ No____

6. Who do you think started the fight?
   Wolfgang____ Oscar____

7. Do you think that both men had tempers? Yes____ No____

8. Do you think that Oscar broke Wolfgang's violin? Yes____ No____

9. Did Wolfgang have a gun?
   Yes____ No____

10. Did Wolfgang have reason to take violent action against Oscar?
    Yes____ No____

11. Reconstruct what probably happened.

Solution on page 59

FOOTSTEPS IN THE DARK

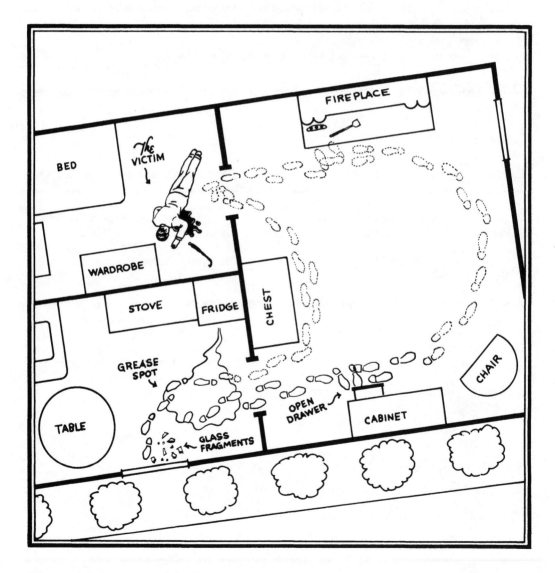

Detective Mercymee's sketch of C. T. Jenny's bungalow is here reproduced. Jenny, a coin collector, had a valuable collection, which is now missing. He was killed by a savage blow from a poker.

The footsteps, made by traversing the grease spot, matched the shoes of a cat burglar known as Meeow. Meeow admitted having been in Jenny's house, but when interrogated he denied killing Jenny and made the statements copied down here. By examining the sketch, can you decide whether Meeow told the truth and was innocent of the Jenny homicide?

Questions

Do you think that the following statements are true, false, or that there is insufficient evidence to support any conclusions?

1. "I busted the kitchen window to get in." True____ False____ Insufficient evidence____

2. "I stop at the kitchen door to give the joint the once-over, but I don't see nothing." True____ False____ Insufficient evidence____

3. "I walk over to the cabinet and yank open a drawer." True____ False____ Insufficient evidence____

4. "I circle the room to kind of see what's what." True____ False____ Insufficient evidence____

5. "In front of the fireplace I stop cold." True____ False____ Insufficient evidence____

6. "Because I see a dead body lying there in the next room." True____ False____ Insufficient evidence____

7. "I want nothing to do with what I see, so I beat it straight out." True____ False____ Insufficient evidence____

8. Do you think that Meeow killed Jenny? Yes____ No____

Solution on page 60

Back to the Classroom

For a time Wilbur Unisex taught a class in investigative techniques at the police school in the local university. In order to test the ability of his students to observe accurately, he gave them the two pictures shown here and asked them to note as many dissimilarities between the two as they could find. Although Wilbur came up with a perfect score, very few of his students located all the discrepancies. (There are twelve.) Can you?

(Note: Some of Wilbur's students claimed that, since he had made the two sketches himself, he knew all the answers. He disdained comment.)

B

Solution on page 60

DROPOUT

As the clock struck five, ninety-year-old Mrs. Mirabel Fallwell dropped out of the window of her spacious twelfth-floor apartment. On the fourth stroke she struck.

Detective Amos Shrewd investigated shortly afterwards and found the room as you see it. Jerry Jarvis, Mrs. Fallwell's nephew and heir, said that the portrait on the wall of his beloved aunt was one that he himself had painted. Under questioning, he claimed that he had been at the far end of the apartment at the time of the tragedy and that he knew nothing about it until informed by the police.

If you were Shrewd, would you charge Jarvis with homicide?

Questions

1. Is there a reason why Mirabel interrupted her phone call and went to the window? Yes____ No____

2. Did Mirabel rush to the window? Yes____ No____

3. Is it likely that she brought a footstool to the window? Yes____ No____

4. Is it reasonable to suppose that Mirabel had a dizzy spell while at the window? Yes____ No____

5. Did she try to keep herself from falling out of the window? Yes____ No____

6. Do you think she committed suicide? Yes____ No____

7. What do you think was the cause of death? Accident____ Murder____

Solution on page 61

BANKWARD HO!

The body of Charles Townsend III was found lying on the floor near his desk, which is shown. He had been shot and killed, and a gun was lying on the floor next to his body.

The elevator boy told the police that around the time Mr. Townsend was believed to have been killed a flashily dressed brunette left the Townsend apartment. According to the elevator boy, she had been a frequent visitor. Subsequently, the police identified her as Ruth L. Frye, a masseuse.

From these facts and an examination of Townsend's desk and the objects on it, can you decide how he met his death?

Questions

1. Do you think that Townsend was having an affair with Mrs. Frye? Yes____ No____

2. Was he in financial straits? Yes____ No____

3. Did he gamble? Yes____ No____

4. Was he a proud man? Yes____ No____

5. Had he formerly been wealthy? Yes____ No____

6. Do you think he robbed a bank? Yes____ No____

7. Had he been drinking alone? Yes____ No____

8. Do you think that he had had a falling out with Mrs. Frye? Yes____ No____

9. How do you think he met his death? Mrs. Frye killed him____ The elevator boy killed him____ He committed suicide____

Solution on page 61

MURDER IN A BOOKSTORE

The Christmas Stra—

82

Suddenly a hood was pulled over h
head with a noose that tightened o
his throat. Unable to see, to call ou
or to breathe, he died quickly. Whe
the body was discovered, it lay on
its back, ankles crossed, and with
happy Santa Claus perched on th
breastbone. The noose was fas
with the same kind of tourn
used in two previous Ch
murders.

On December 23rd the body of Quintus Tertius, a bibliophile, was found as shown in the basement of the Boswell Bookstore. Page 82 of *The Christmas Strangler,* by Elden Hack, lay open on a counter. Mr. Tertius, a regular customer, often rummaged in the stacks of books in the basement.

Eppis Pepys and his wife, Alice Pepys, were proprietors of the Boswell Bookstore. Each of them admitted having gone down to the basement within a half hour of the probable time of the murder.

E. Pepys said, "I went down to get a copy of Descartes's *Principles of Philosophy.* I saw no one in the basement."

A. Pepys said, "I went down to get a copy of Spinoza's *Ethics.* I saw no one in the basement."

From these facts and from an examination of scene, can you tell who killed Quintus Tertius, and why?

Questions

1. Did Tertius commit suicide? Yes___ No___

2. Is it likely that the murderer entered and left the bookstore without being noticed? Yes___ No___

3. Do you think Tertius was reading *The Christmas Strangler* when he was accosted? Yes___ No___

4. Did the murder method require preparation? Yes___ No___

5. Do you think the killer brought his murder equipment with him? Yes___ No___

6. Did Eppis Pepys have a motive for killing Tertius? Yes___ No___

7. Did Alice Pepys have a motive for killing Tertius? Yes___ No___

8. Do you think that the killer brought *The Christmas Strangler* with him? Yes___ No___

9. Do you think that Tertius was engrossed in reading at the time of his murder? Yes___ No___

10. Can you figure out a probable motive for this murder?

11. Who do you think killed Tertius?

Solution on page 62

SNOW COVER

Eli P. Harvard was found dead inside his ski lodge, which is shown. A revolver was clutched in his hand and a bullet from it had entered his head at close range, killing him instantly.

Detective Boozle, trying to decide whether Eli had committed suicide or been murdered, learned that Eli had spent the night with Sally Merrybottom, his girl friend, had phoned three of his friends the next morning to tell them that he'd finally broken off with Sally after a rather tempestuous scene, and that she'd promised to leave the house during the morning while he went skiing. Early that afternoon all three friends, worried and unable to reach him by phone, called the police, who arrived and immediately roped off all footprints and other marks that they found in the snow.

It had snowed for an hour or so that morning, and consequently the tracks that you see were made on the day of the tragedy. The footprints other than those fenced off were made by the police themselves, who entered the lodge through the back door, which is not shown.

If you were Boozle, what conclusions would you draw?

Questions

1. Does the fact that Eli died with a revolver in his hand prove that he committed suicide? Yes_____ No_____

2. Do you think he had been skiing? Yes_____ No_____

3. Are the footprints Sally's? Yes_____ No_____

4. Did Sally have a motive for murder? Yes_____ No_____

5. Were any of the ski marks made before the footprints? Yes_____ No_____

6. Do Sally's footprints indicate that she left before Eli's return? Yes_____ No_____

7. Insofar as you know, did Eli have a motive for committing suicide? Yes_____ No_____

8. Do you think Sally shot him? Yes_____ No_____

9. Based on the evidence of the sketch, reconstruct what happened as well as you can.

Solution on page 63

KIDNAP

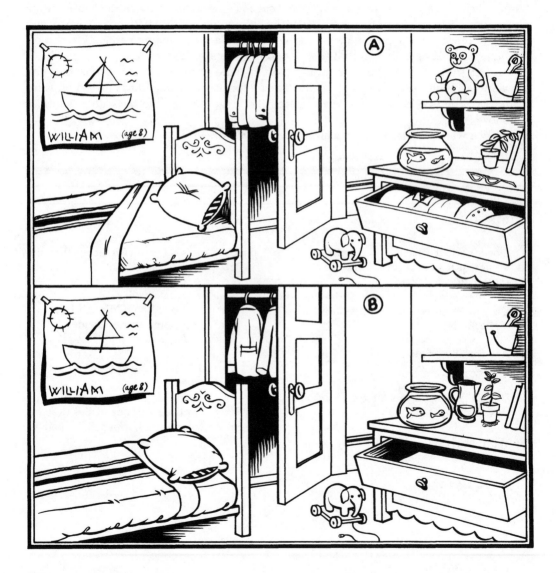

Sketch A shows eight-year-old William's room as it was just before his loving mother put him to bed for his afternoon nap, and Sketch B shows the room as it was an hour later, after she'd finished her daily meditation and reported to Sergeant Foxxy that William was missing. Foxxy made a preliminary examination, concluded that William had been kidnapped, and listed the following suspects:

- William's loving father, who was having a custody fight with William's loving mother and had threatened to abduct his son;
- Martha Soul, who had been William's loving nurse for the past several years, but had had to leave a week ago because William's loving mother could no longer afford a nurse;
- Mr. Green, the gardener who had been working here for the last three months;
- William's loving mother.
  Which one of the four do you think Foxxy should accuse?

Questions

1. Did young William leave willingly?
   Yes____ No____

2. Was young William neat?
   Yes____ No____

3. Did young William's loving mother have a motive for taking him from his room? Yes____ No____

4. Did his loving father have a motive for kidnapping him? Yes____ No____

5. Did the gardener have a motive for kidnapping him? Yes____ No____

6. Did his loving nurse have a motive for kidnapping him? Yes____ No____

7. Did the kidnapper water the plant?
   Yes____ No____

8. Was the kidnapper familiar with the house? Yes____ No____

9. Did the kidnapper intend to hold William for more than a day or two?
   Yes____ No____

10. Was the loving mother likely to hear the kidnapper at work?
    Yes____ No____

11. Do you think the loving father kidnapped William? Yes____ No____

12. Do you think the gardener kidnapped William? Yes____ No____

13. Do you think William's mother was the kidnapper and that she secreted William where his loving father couldn't find him? Yes____ No____

14. Do you think William's loving nurse kidnapped him? Yes____ No____

Solution on page 63

39

BOY SCOUT

At about four o'clock in the afternoon a group of hikers came upon this scene at the top of a cliff. At about the same time another group of hikers found the body of C. C. Robin at the base of the same cliff. He had been killed by a heavy blow on the head, and was wearing one boot only.

Four people were known to have been on the scene at some time between two o'clock and four o'clock. The four people were:

- C. C. Robin, the distinguished ornithologist, out for a day trip;
- Arch Forrester, a game warden with a temper;
- Little Nimrod, a poacher with a bad reputation;
- Bernie Botchett, on his first camping trip.

On the basis of the above facts, plus an examination of the scene, can you figure out who killed C. C. Robin?

Questions

1. Had Robin's body been dragged to the edge of the cliff?
   Yes_____ No_____

2. Is it legal to shoot an eagle?
   Yes_____ No_____

3. Do you think that the eagle was shot before Forrester reached the scene?
   Yes_____ No_____

4. Is there evidence of a fight?
   Yes_____ No_____

5. Which two of the four men do you think had the fight? Robin_____
   Forrester_____ Little Nimrod_____
   Botchett_____

6. What murder weapons were available for use?

7. Had someone made preparations to camp out? Yes_____ No_____

8. Who do you think chopped at the tree? Robin_____ Forrester_____ Little Nimrod_____ Botchett_____

9. Who do you think sat down and drank beer together? Robin_____ Forrester_____ Little Nimrod_____ Botchett_____

10. Do you think that the camper left hurriedly? Yes_____ No_____

11. Who do you think killed Robin? Forrester_____ Little Nimrod_____ Botchett_____

12. Can you describe what probably happened?

Solution on page 64

THE MAN IN 1458

A man whose appearance nobody remembered registered at the Withered Arms as John Smith. He occupied this room for a few days and left with an unpaid bill of over $500.00. As a police officer assigned to locate him, what do you know about him and how accurately can you identify him on the basis of the objects shown?

Questions

1. Was the Withered Arms a large hotel? Yes_____ No_____

2. Do you think that the occupant's name was John Smith? Yes_____ No_____

3. Was he tall? Yes_____ No_____

4. Was he left-handed? Yes_____ No_____

5. Did he have a mustache? Yes_____ No_____

6. About how old was he?

7. Was he well groomed? Yes_____ No_____

8. Was he neat? Yes_____ No_____

9. Do you think he was a foreigner? Yes_____ No_____

10. Was he broke? Yes_____ No_____

11. Did he intend to cheat the hotel when he registered? Yes_____ No_____

12. What steps could the hotel take to apprehend him?

Solution on page 65

GANG OF FOUR

Burglars broke a window and entered the home of Samuel F. Whippersnapper, a coin collector, and rifled his collection. He grappled with them and was shot and fatally wounded in the course of the struggle. He had time, however, to call the police, who stopped a car with these four suspects in it and brought them to the station house, together with the coat, which had some of the stolen coins in a pocket.

Whippersnapper died clutching the button which is shown. The police were satisfied that the other objects sketched, which were found at Whippersnapper's, belonged to the burglars. From the above facts and an examination of the evidence and the four suspects, can you decide who shot Whippersnapper?

Questions

1. Who do you think broke the window?
   Dan Jurous_____ "Bull" Dozer_____
   Helen Wheels_____ "Brains" B.
   Heind_____

2. At what time did the struggle occur?

3. Do you think that more than one person was involved in the burglary?
   Yes_____ No_____

4. Does the button come from the coat found in the car? Yes_____ No_____

5. Do you think that "Bull" Dozer was involved in the struggle?
   Yes_____ No_____

6. Do you think that the wearer of the coat killed Whippersnapper?
   Yes_____ No_____

7. Who do you think shot Whippersnapper? Dan Jurous_____ "Bull" Dozer_____ Helen Wheels_____ "Brains" B. Heind_____

Solution on page 66

An 8¢ Story

The day after Georgio Erysipelas lost fifteen dollars and eight cents to Hans Liverwurst in their weekly poker game, Georgio entered Hans's High Class Delicatessen. Both men were known to be short tempered and had previously come close to fighting over poker hands, but this time the fight was to the death, as Hans's body attests.

All that Detective Sharpeye could learn from witnesses who had heard the argument leading to the tragedy was that Georgio had shouted out in English, "That's all you'll get!" Hans had responded angrily in German, whereupon Georgio had switched into high gear, but in Greek.

Can you guess what they accused each other of?

Questions

1. Was Hans apparently eating when Georgio came into the store?
   Yes ____ No ____

2. Whose footprints are shown?
   Hans's ____ Georgio's ____

3. Did Hans stop at the pickle barrel?
   Yes ____ No ____

4. Do you think Hans offered Georgio a pickle? Yes ____ No ____

5. Do you think Hans and Georgio were on friendly terms when Georgio entered the store? Yes ____ No ____

6. Did Hans return to his table at any time after leaving it?
   Yes ____ No ____

7. Do you think that Georgio came to pay his debt? Yes ____ No ____

8. Do you think that Georgio came to the store with malice aforethought?
   Yes ____ No ____

9. Is there any evidence to show that Georgio may have acted in self-defense? Yes ____ No ____

10. Where did the murder weapon come from?

11. Do you think Hans objected to the fact that the five dollar bill was torn?
    Yes ____ No ____

12. What do you think the argument was about: The 8¢ ____ The pickles ____ The $10.00 ____

Solution on page 67

WEDDING DAY

After a night on the town with a few friends, young Lochinvar woke up in his bedroom on a gray, sunless morn and faced his wedding day as you see it. He was known to be compulsively late on practically all occasions, and the lovely Griselda, his bride-to-be, had said that if he was as much as one minute late for their 11:00 A.M. ceremony, the marriage would be off.

If you were young Lochinvar, what would you do?

Solution on page 68

SOLUTIONS

Solution to *Boudoir* (p.2)

1. Strangled, with the kerchief which is still around her neck.

2. No. All objects are apparently in place.

3. Yes, strong enough to overpower and strangle her, and to bend the bars of the bird cage.

4. Yes. She is wearing a bracelet, and her jewel box is overflowing with jewelry.

5. No, because her jewelry was left in its box, and there is no indication of a search for valuables.

6. Yes, because there is no sign of a struggle, and she was apparently still brushing her hair when attacked.

7. No. If the bird had been strangled while she was still alive, she would have objected forcibly and not simply have sat there brushing her hair.

8. Yes. The killer was angered enough to strangle both Amy and her bird.

9. Yes. It was jealousy, aroused by the sight of Joe's picture and his gifts.

10. Henry Willy, because Spanker would have stolen, Wonty seems to have been in good favor, and the maid had no reason to kill and probably lacked the strength to strangle Amy and break the bars of the cage.

Solution to *Fragment* (p. 4)

1. Yes, because he is addressed as Gam in line 12.

2. Yes, because in line 3 she refers to his return.

3. Yes. Lovey says in line 12 that he's dangerous, and in line 5 she speaks of jealousy.

4. Yes. The theater stub gives part of a phone number (5000) such as is usually assigned to hotels and public buildings, and the other digits probably refer to a room number.

5. Yes. In line 14 she alludes to an address being "c/o my sister," and then gives an address—a measure taken to prevent Ordway's letters from arriving at Lovey's apartment. Furthermore she refers to the butler delivering something—probably this very letter—a measure she must have taken to deceive her husband.

6. Yes. She refers to a theater ticket from yesterday, which was June 7, the day before the date of the letter, which is June 8. (June is the only month that ends in "e".)

7. See below.

8. Yes. He had a motive, he had the means of discovering Ordway's hotel room, he had a theater stub which (line 10) he apparently took from Lovey's evening bag and which was found in Ordway's room, thus placing Lovey's husband there. He apparently faced Ordway in a rage and accused him of an affair with Lovey. The rest is history.

THE LETTER:

June 8
Gam darling —
    My husband is back! He came late last night, in a taxi direct from the Pennsylvania station. He was terribly upset and jealous because of the gossip he'd heard. Luckily he doesn't know your name, but he found the stub of the theatre ticket from yesterday —the one on which you wrote your phone and room no.—in my evening bag, and he took it, swearing he'd find and kill the man I was with. It's terrible. Oh, Gam, he's dangerous and hot tempered. You must promise to go away at once. You can write me c/o my sister— Mrs. Annie Laurel, at 115 Wyckoff Place. I'm so afraid, and simply worried to death. I'm sending this to you by hand—the butler's delivering it—because John mustn't find you.

        Your,
        Lovey

Solution to *End of a Villain* (p. 6)

1. No. The rod looks unused, and there is no evidence of bait or lures.

2. Yes. The broken oar, the missing oarlock, the spilled paint, and the potpourri of feet indicate trouble.

3. No. There is no suicide note, and a man bent on suicide would neither engage in a fight nor plant evidence of one. He would want to go without fuss or fury.

4. No. It is flat-bottomed.

5. No. This would not explain the broken oar and missing oarlock, nor the footprints.

6. Yes. The cut is clean, and it would be difficult to break this kind of tough neoprene.

7. Yes. There is no apparent need for paint.

8. Yes, because there are two distinctly different shoe patterns marking the bottom of the boat, one of which was made by a left shoe only and must have been deliberately planted, the other of which must have been made by the person planting the left shoe-prints.

9. One, for reasons cited in (8).

10. Romano apparently planted evidence of a fight and then disappeared voluntarily, probably with all the money he could gather and with the intention of starting a new life.

   Actually he did exactly that, and was killed a year later by a Chicago prostitute whose services he tried to get for nothing.

Solution to *Merrill's Alibi* (p. 8)

1. Yes. Judging by his trophies, he was obviously an athlete.

2. Yes. The gun rack indicates he was interested in gunnery, and as an athlete he may well have been a marksman.

3. No, because apparently one gun is missing.

4. Yes, because it places him at his apartment at 6:45 P.M., so that it would have been impossible for him to reach the Allen estate at seven, when the murder occurred.

5. No, because their stories are inconsistent with each other.

6. Yes, because she mentions the poetry volume and the broken bulb.

7. No. Nothing in the room is inconsistent with her story.

8. Yes, because his umbrella is wet.

9. "I was reading it when you people came in." This cannot be true because at 7:40 on a November evening there would not be enough natural light by which to read a paper in the chair Merrill claimed to have been sitting in. Had he been reading, he would have sat in the chair at the right, after moving the package.

10. Yes. Merrill had a motive, he was a good shot and an athlete, and he fabricated an alibi containing a falsehood. Actually he shot Ferris Allen at long range, then rushed home and pretended to be reading the paper when the police came in. Euphrosyne mourned briefly, but she never forgave Merrill for his stupidity in sitting in the wrong chair. Shortly after Merrill's conviction for murder, she married the judge.

Solution to *A Matter of Diamonds* (p. 10)

1. At C. As hostess, she poured the tea.

2. At B, judging by his prescription pad, on which he doodled and jotted down the figure of $55,000.00.

3. Yes, judging by the way he doodled on his prescription pad and then crumpled a sheet from it.

4. No. Judging by the flag, which is hanging limp, it was not a windy day.

5. No. She might have been a kleptomaniac, or in need of cash despite her wealth.

6. No. Mrs. Dogge and the doctor pushed their settings away from them, as if propping themselves up and then jumping back to run, whereas Weimaraner pulled his setting towards him, as if scooping something up and yanking it towards him.

7. Weimaraner, who took them in the hope of collecting insurance money. The proof is contained in the answer to Question 6. Weimaraner, when searched, claimed that the diamonds found on him were not the diamonds that he had been showing, but Wilbur Unisex's theory of the scoop was unrefutable. In gratitude to Wilbur for having eased what was an awkward situation, Mrs. Dogge invited him to dinner.

Solution to *The Van Bliven Necklace* (p. 12)

1. A, because the clock indicates an earlier time than in B.

2. Yes, because her suitcase is out on the floor.

3. The jewel box (open), the bureau drawer (open), and the suitcase (moved, with one of the catches left open).

4. No, because she would not have heard the phone ring while it was unplugged.

5. No, because the broken glass lies outside the room.

6. No, only if he had broken a window from the inside of Mrs. Van Bliven's room to unlock the doors, which would have been impossible.

7. No. She had legitimate reasons for entering the room, such as bringing towels and turning down the bed for the night.

8. Yes, because the bed covers are turned down.

9. No, because if she had stolen the necklace she would have avoided making any noise or leaving evidence of her presence.

54

10. Yes. She could easily have manufactured all the evidence present.

11. In the vase, because the flowers were moved, and there seems to have been no other reason for rearranging or tampering with them.

12. Mrs. Van Bliven, because we have eliminated the other two suspects, and she could have recovered the necklace from the vase at any time she wished. Due to her craving for caviar and the money she'd spent for it, she was badly in need of cash. "Caviar was my downfall!" she cried out as she was led away by the police.

Solution to *Dead Man's Curvature* (p. 14)

1. Yes, as proved by the tire marks.

2. Yes. She stood to collect $300,000.00.

3. Yes, because Dicky was apparently having an affair with Daniel V's wife.

4. Yes, because Daniel V. defended Ellie and called her by her first name.

5. No, judging by the nature of the breaks, in which the upper part of each fence rail was sawed cleanly, and the bottom part broken off.

6. Yes. The tire marks show that it backed up to avoid going over the rock, and it had to stop before it could back up.

7. Yes. We already know that he did not crash through the fence. It is hard to believe that he stopped at the break in the fence, backed up to avoid the rock, and then drove the few feet over the edge of the cliff. If he'd wanted to go over, he'd have done so at a goodly clip, and without hesitation.

8. Yes, because whoever drove Dicky's car to the fence needed a confederate to help him leave the scene. The tire marks at the left of the road indicate that there was such a confederate in a second car.

9. Ellie and Daniel V. conspired to kill Dicky. In Answer 8 we found out that two people were involved. One of them had to cut the fence, which could probably have been done without arousing suspicion, and the second person had to drive the car to the fence.

   The facts are that, inasmuch as nobody questions what a workman is doing, Daniel V. felt perfectly safe in driving to the spot in the road known as Dead Man's Curvature, parking on the opposite side of the road, and proceeding to cut the fence down. Meanwhile Ellie had killed Dicky at home, and, with his body sharing the front seat with her, drove to the rendezvous with Daniel V. She stopped with one wheel in front of the rock and had to back up so that she and her paramour could then push the car over the edge of the cliff and drive off together.

As for Ronda Ravish, she waited for Dicky all night long, and in the morning she had to pay the bill.

Solution to *Tragedy in the Bathroom* (p. 16)

1. No. Judging by the towels, he was neat, and she was sloppy. (If you decide that the evidence is inconclusive, your answer is not incorrect, since they might have been compatible on other levels.)

2. No, because his toothbrush still has a ribbon of toothpaste on it and the neatly rolled and capped tube lies on the sink's rim.

3. Yes, because the shower floor is wet.

4. No, because his feet are dry.

5. Yes, because her wet shoeprint exits from the shower.

6. No. Although the soap is standing in a puddle, Horace's feet are dry. Furthermore, there are no slippage marks to show that the soap slid or skidded.

7. No, because it would have fallen onto the floor of the shower stall rather than to its present position.

8. No. It is too far away from both. Therefore the soap and puddle must have been positioned deliberately.

9. No, because he would not have stood barefoot near a broken bottle.

10. Yes. The heavy scales are far enough out of balance to indicate that they had sustained a heavy jar.

11. Yes. The shower has been turned on and off although Horace took no shower, and there are two puddles of no apparent source on the floor outside the shower.

12. Horace was leaning over to brush his teeth when he was hit on the head with the bathroom scales. As he fell, he knocked over a bottle. Minnie then turned on the shower and doused water over Horace's head to make it look as if he'd just showered. To get the soap, on which he had supposedly slipped, she had to step inside the shower stall. She did this with her shoes on and thus left shoeprints.

    In actuality this is what occurred, and Minnie was arrested and eventually confessed. "I couldn't stand the guy's neatness," she said coyly.

Solution to *Check It* (p. 18)

1. Yes, judging by the notations on his calendar.

2. Yes, to prevent Louis from disinheriting him.

3. Yes, for the same reason as in Answer 2.

4. Yes, both had cleared and were stamped as paid.

5. Yes.

6. Yes, the $5000.00 check. Signatures are never absolutely identical unless copied or traced, and one would be unlikely to forge a check for $50.00 when he had a genuine check for one hundred times that amount.

7. Hemini, because if Gemini had killed his father, he, Gemini, would have removed the incriminating check, whereas Hemini might well have been glad to leave it.

8. Hemini, because he was the last person to have seen his father, as indicated in Answer 7. However, the world being what it is and there being no direct evidence to connect Hemini with his crime, the D.A. dropped all charges. Accused of dereliction of his duty, he said that his higher obligation of protecting the public had been performed because, now that Hemini had killed his father, he would never do it again.

   It should be noted that, if Louis had kept his thoughts to himself, he could be alive today.

Solution to *The Lunchroom Murder* (p. 20)

1. Yes, because the pail, mop, and wet floor so indicate.

2. Four, because there are four checks, plates, cups, and sets of cutlery.

3. No, because the money has not been taken from the cash drawer.

4. Yes, because their three checks totaling $8.75 were rung up together on the cash register. It follows that one of them treated the other two. The fact they they sat next to each other is not convincing, although it is indicative.

5. No, because D has finished eating and has paid; A has done neither.

6. At least six—A, B, C, D, Ernie and Fannin.

7. No. They leave no mark on a dry floor.

8. Y, because they start from near the mop which only he would be using

and then proceed to the cash drawer which only he would open, except in case of robbery, which we know has not occurred in this instance.

9. No, because only his toe marks show, indicating that he ran.

10. Yes, because his footsteps (heel and toe mark) show that he walked and did not run to the cash register.

11. Near the cash register, because we know that he walked to it and ran from it, and because he did not close the cash drawer. It follows that something—namely the murder—frightened him while he was there.

12. Z, because they start at the far side of stool A.

13. Yes, because his toe marks leave via the kitchen door.

14. Yes, because the man whose handprint appears must have stood near the mop, in the position where footprints X appear.

15. No, because the mark of his right hand appears on the wall. Therefore he held the gun in his left hand.

16. C, because he was left-handed. Cups are normally placed at the right and *are* at the right of A's, B's, and D's plates. C's cup is to the left of his plate. It follows that C was left-handed and the murderer.

Solution to *Extortion* (p. 22)

1. Yes, because the letter was mailed to him.

2. No, because there are no foreign mannerisms or letter combinations. The threat is written in colloquial but fluent English.

3. Yes, because he forgot himself twice and spelled "you" correctly; because the misspelling is overdone, with difficult words such as "Josephine," "pocketbook," and "desperado" spelled correctly; and because paragraphing and punctuation are correct throughout.

4. Yes, because it is not the letter of a person unable to write in longhand, as has been brought out in Answer 3.

5. No, because he was apparently able to enter the public writing rooms of the Ritz-Plaza hotel.

6. No, because the tone of the letter is amateurish (see, for example, the signature), and because the amount demanded is extremely small.

7. Yes, because no means are provided for Nutmeg's identification.

8. Yes, because he apparently knew Nutmeg's habit of walking to his mother's on Tuesdays.

9. Yes, because he evidently knew the floor and frontage of Nutmeg's bedroom.

10. No, because the writer specified a particular petit-point pocketbook but did not demand that it be wrapped. Had the writer been a man, he would have insisted on having the pocketbook wrapped up lest it make him conspicuous at a time when he did not want to be noticed.

11. A discharged governess, because it was a woman familiar with Nutmeg's apartment, his habits, and his wife's pocketbook, and a woman who found it necessary to pretend a lack of education. It is not the Irish chambermaid because she would probably not have used the word "denominations," and it is not the waitress because she would not be familiar with the apartment, Nutmeg's habits, or the pocketbook.

Solution to *Music Hath Charms* (p. 24)

1. Yes, judging by the jack-in-the-box, the masks, and the whoopee cushion.

2. Oscar's, because Wolfgang would not be likely to have his jacket hanging next to the door. He would probably have it in his own closet elsewhere.

3. Yes, judging by the fine wines catalogue in his coat pocket.

4. Yes. It probably costs from $35.00 up, depending on the year.

5. Yes. Wolfgang apparently played a cheap trick on him by pretending to serve him Chateau Lafite, when it was obvious from the shape of the bottle (Burgundy wine bottle shaped) that the wine in it was not a Bordeaux wine, as Lafite is.

6. Oscar, because he probably resented the trick.

7. Yes, judging by the destruction in the room.

8. Yes. Wolfgang would never break his own violin.

9. Yes. Since there was a box of cartridges in the open drawer of the table, it follows that there had probably been a gun there also.

10. Yes, because Oscar had broken the violin, which probably cost thousands of dollars and was irreplaceable.

11. In all likelihood Oscar accused Wolfgang of trying to play a cheap trick on him, Wolfgang resented the accusation, they tangled, and in the course of the struggle Oscar broke Wolfgang's violin. This was unforgivable. Wolfgang went for his gun, and in the struggle both men were shot.

   It is rumored that both of them are learning to play the harp, although their progress is questionable.

Solution to *Footsteps in the Dark* (p. 26)

1. True, because of the broken glass on the floor near the window, unless there was a mysterious someone else—which you may discount.

2. True, judging by the footsteps.

3. True, judging by the footsteps and the open drawer.

4. True, judging by the footsteps.

5. True, judging by the footsteps.

6. Insufficient evidence. We do not know what he saw at this point, whether it was Jenny or his dead body or something else. We merely know that he did stop.

7. False, because his footsteps show that he entered the bedroom.

8. Yes. Most of Meeow's statements are irrelevant to his guilt, but whether or not he entered the bedroom is crucial. Since he lied about this, he is suspect, and the suspicion is confirmed by his having stopped at the fireplace, where he can be assumed to have picked up the poker.

   Subsequent to Meeow's interrogation, the poker was brought to the technical laboratory, where it was found to be the murder weapon and to have Meeow's latent prints on it. He then confessed, and told everyone that a cat burglar should never rob on the ground floor, since he is made for a higher purpose.

Solution to *Back to the Classroom* (p. 28)

1. There are no rays around the sun in B.

2. Smoke comes from the chimney in B.

3. The pump handle is scalloped in B.

4. The final "e" is missing from "severe" in the sign next to the pump in B.

5. The position of the envelope near Maudie's left foot is slightly different in B.

6. The cup of the ladle is different in B.

7. The well cover is built from six planks in A and five in B.

8. The bucket handle is missing in B.

9. The letter in Maudie's hand is signed "Horace" in A and "Homer" in B.

10. Maudie's right shoe is missing in B.

11. The flower near Maudie's right elbow has two leaves in A and one leaf in B.

12. There are three flowers just above the envelope in A and two flowers in B.

Solution to *Dropout* (p. 30)

1. Yes. She must have heard the blare and scream of the fire engines and gone to the window to watch the proceedings.

2. No. She took the time to prop her memo pad against the phone, and probably to bring the footstool to the window.

3. Yes, because she was a short woman (study her portrait and compare her height to that of the six-foot-six doorway), and she obviously wanted to see all that she could.

4. Yes, for three reasons. First, because she was looking down from a height and might have suffered from vertigo; second, because at the age of ninety she might very well have been subject to dizzy spells; and third, because she had been drinking sherry and might have been slightly intoxicated.

5. Yes. She apparently grabbed at the curtain, which tore from her weight as she fell.

6. No. There was no suicide note, and she was apparently in the middle of the normal act of phoning when she got up and went to the window.

7. Murder, because if she'd fallen accidentally, her weight would have been on the front of the footstool and it would have fallen forward, with the top towards the window and the legs towards the viewer. Since the legs face the window, it follows that the footstool was deliberately placed in its present position, probably to mislead the police. Jarvis, however, made the fatal error of the footstool.
   He is said to have regretted his mistake.

Solution to *Bankward Ho!* (p. 32)

1. Yes, because he'd bought her expensive clothes and expensive jewelry.

2. You bet!

3. Yes. He had winnings at bridge.

4. Yes, because he paid his club dues and his son's tuition while he was still solvent. Most of his other checks bounced.

5. Yes, judging by the facts that he belonged to a private club and sent his son to a private school.

6. Yes. Where else could he obtain packages of bills neatly fastened together?

7. Yes, judging by the single glass and the nearly empty bottle.

8. Yes, because she apparently returned her bracelet and brooch, and because either he or she smashed her picture, as if in anger.

9. Ruth would not have killed Townsend and then left her brooch and bracelet, and the elevator boy would not have killed him and left the money. It follows that Townsend committed suicide, as he had every reason to—he was broke, his girl had left him, he'd robbed a bank and faced arrest, and he'd been drinking alone, as if in deep despair.

Solution to *Murder in a Bookstore* (p. 34)

1. No. You can't strangle yourself with a tourniquet. Don't try it!

2. Yes. December 23rd was at the height of the Christmas rush, when bookstores are crowded. Any bookseller can expand on the ordeal.

3. No. This was a non-fiction area frequented more by bibliophiles than mystery readers, and *Hagiology,* by Gregory Pope, lay open near the victim's hand, suggesting that he was reading this book when attacked by the murderer.

4. Yes. This is obvious from the presence of the tourniquet, the hood, and the gloating little Santa Claus, which are not objects ordinarily taken on a trip to a bookstore.

5. Yes. The opened package next to the body indicates how the murderer brought his equipment here.

6. No. You don't kill your customers. This is a rule that all booksellers follow faithfully.

7. No, for the reasons cited in (6).

8. Yes. This is a non-fiction area, where mystery novels would feel unwanted.

9. Yes. Otherwise it would have been difficult to throw a hood over him without leaving evidence of a fight.

10. Yes, publicity for the book.

11. Elden Hack, in order to get publicity for his book, which it got. And so did he.

Solution to *Snow Cover* (p. 36)

1. No. The revolver could have been put in his hand after he'd been shot.

2. Yes. The marks of his skis and ski poles are clear in the snow.

3. Yes, because no one else was in the house except Eli, who left and returned on skis.

4. Yes. It is well known that discarded mistresses are inclined to kill.

5. Yes, because some of the boot marks are superimposed on the ski marks.

6. Yes, because Eli's returning ski marks are superimposed on Sally's shoes or boots.

7. No. He'd just gotten rid of a woman he didn't want, and he'd been sufficiently elated over it to tell three of his friends.

8. Yes. Since he did not commit suicide, she must have shot him.

9. After Eli had left, Sally must have walked out, then put on boots and returned, but walking backwards and obliterating her earlier marks. Thus she gave the superficial impression of having left the house, but closer examination shows that the heel marks are deeper than the toe marks as weight was put on the heel in the course of moving. There is always a pushing movement in the direction of motion. Furthermore some snow is kicked up in the direction of passage, leaving a fuzzy edge. Compare Sally's boot marks with those of the police, who were walking normally, and the difference is clear.

   Actually Sally was waiting in the house when Eli returned. She shot him and then hid in the cellar, from which she hoped to escape at the first opportunity. Boozle, however, was too smart for her and found her cowering in the wine cellar, slightly drunk.

Solution to *Kidnap* (p. 38)

1. Yes, because he took his teddy bear and some clothes, and there are no signs of a struggle.

2. Yes. His room is reasonably neat, so he was probably a neat child.

3. Yes, to prevent her husband from kidnapping William.

4. Yes, to obtain custody of William, which was denied by the loving mother.

5. Yes. He could have obtained ransom money.

6. Yes. She was probably lonesome for him.

7. Yes, judging by the spilled water near the base of the pot.

8. Yes. The kidnapper found the pitcher and went about routine tasks like making the bed, filling the fish bowl, and watering the plant.

9. Yes, because his teddy bear and clothes were taken.

10. No. She was apparently deep in meditation.

11. No. He would have been in hostile territory and would have had to act quickly, and would never have wasted time over the plant and the fishbowl, nor would he have made the bed.

12. No. He should not have been in the house and he, like the loving father, would have worked fast.

13. No. She would not have bothered taking clothes, because she had continual access to them.

14. Yes. She was familiar with the house, she could act slowly, and if discovered she could claim that she'd returned for her glasses, or some other item. She would do familiar chores such as making the bed, filling the fish bowl, and watering the plant.

   Actually, she took William and returned him after two days, because he ate so much and she couldn't afford to feed him.

Solution to *Boy Scout* (p. 40)

1. Yes, the marks and the lost boot so indicate.

2. No, no, a thousand times no.

3. No. Otherwise the game warden would have taken the dead eagle with him as evidence of the illegal act. He must have arrived at and left the scene before the eagle was deposited there.

4. Yes. There is a depression in the thorny bushes where twigs and branches were broken, as if somebody fell and tore his shirt, a fragment of which caught on a thorn.

5. Little Nimrod and Robin. We have already seen that Forrester had left the scene early, and it is likely that Robin, an ornithologist, would accuse Little Nimrod of killing the eagle. A fight could, and did result, after which Little Nimrod left hurriedly without his eagle.

6. We know that someone had an ax, judging by the nicked tree, and that Nimrod had a gun.

7. Yes, the makings of a fire and the tent pegs so indicate.

8. Botchett, because this is a botched job by an inexperienced camper. Both Little Nimrod and Forrester were probably expert woodsmen, and Robin would have had no reason to chop wood.

9. Botchett (he had the equipment, and probably a supply of beer) and Robin, who left his binoculars where he'd been drinking. And binoculars are standard equipment for a birder.

10. Yes. He left some of his food and some of his possessions, including a plate and the tent pegs.

11. Botchett. We have already decided that both Little Nimrod and Forrester had left the scene.

12. Botchett, an inexpert camper, was chopping wood, and the ax must have slipped out of his hands, which is an all-too-common happening with the inexperienced. A flying ax is a murderous weapon, and there is no reason to think that Botchett would attack Robin.

In actuality Botchett got rid of the body by pushing it over the edge of the cliff. When he heard the sounds of hikers, he packed up his tent and his ax and left in a hurry, leaving tell-tale evidence of his presence.

Solution to *The Man in 1458* (p. 42)

1. Yes. Judging by the room number, the hotel had at least fourteen floors with fifty-eight or more rooms per floor.

2. No. It is a common alias, and, combined with other factors here, it is doubtful that this was his real name.

3. Yes. One usually writes at eye level, which is about five inches below actual height. Because of the perspective of this drawing, it is impossible to measure "John Smith's" exact height, but a good guess based on the facts that the average door is six-and-a-half feet high and that the top of the switch plate is about four feet above the floor would bring him to at least six feet.

4. Yes. A right-handed man would have had to lean awkwardly over the bureau in order to write on the mirror; and would write at an angle. A tall, left-handed man would naturally stand next to the bureau and scrawl a note on the mirror as the easiest way to jot down a notation of train time, and his writing would be on a line parallel to the top of the mirror.

5. Yes, judging by the mustache brush.

6. Elderly, judging by the half-rate ticket, which is the type given to senior citizens by various common carriers, such as bus, rail, and ferry lines.

7. Yes. He apparently cleaned his shoes (note the used shoe rag); was addicted to bow ties (which are associated with a certain fastidiousness of dress); and travelled with an electric shaver, which he discarded because it was broken.

8. No. He dumped a partly open case on the floor, scattered objects on the bureau, and draped a dirty shoe-rag over the foot of the bed.

9. Yes. He was a foreigner because he crossed the stems of his digit sevens, and because he had a shaver with foreign prongs that needed an adapter for use in American electrical outlets.

10. No. He left a ten-dollar tip for the chambermaid.

11. Yes, because he checked into the hotel with a cheap case stuffed with paper or rags, and with a phone book for weight. Obviously he intended to donate the case to the Withered Arms.

12. In cooperation with the local police, they could contact the conductor of a 3:40 train and give him a description of the man in 1458: well-dressed and possibly wearing a bow tie, foreign, probably speaks with an accent, about six feet tall, elderly, left-handed, has a mustache but no beard, and carries no baggage. The local police would then contact the police at the station where, according to the conductor, the man who matched this description left the train.

    In actuality the man was Abdul Kontacket, a bigamist fleeing from the wrath of beautiful Wife Number Five. He was arrested, and when she was brought into his presence, she threw her arms around him and kissed him passionately. The police had to use force to separate them.

Solution to *Gang of Four* (p. 44)

1. Dan Jurous, because his hand is bandaged.

2. At nine o'clock, judging by the time when the watch stopped.

3. Yes, because a number of items probably belonging to the four people arrested were found at the scene.

4. Yes, because it matches, and a button is missing from the coat.

5. Yes, because the untanned area of his forearm indicates he had been wearing a watch—probably the one found at the scene.

6. Yes, because the coat has a bullet hole, as if the wearer had the gun in his pocket and shot through it.

7. Helen Wheels, because she is the only woman and the coat with the bullet hole is a woman's, judging by the fact that the buttons are on the left-hand side and the button holes on the right. And if that's ever changed, what's left?

Solution to *An 8¢ Story* (p. 46)

1. Yes, judging by the half-finished meal at the table, and by the fact that he kept his napkin on.

2. Hans's, because they come from the table where he was eating.

3. Yes, judging by the footprints.

4. Yes, because he stopped at the napkin holder, and there are two wrapped and half-eaten pickles on the counter.

5. Yes, because Hans offered Georgio a pickle.

6. No. Footprints would have indicated his return.

7. Yes, because the approximate amount of the debt is there on the counter, and it is unlikely that they would have argued over eight cents.

8. No. There is no indication that he carried a weapon or did anything other than proffer fifteen dollars.

9. Yes. Hans left his table with a knife in his hand, and was still holding it when he was killed. He may well have brandished it and threatened with it during the course of the argument.

10. From the roast, because the hilt of the knife matches the hilt of the fork which is still in the roast.

11. No. As a storekeeper he must have been given torn bills many times and he was used to accepting them, provided all the pieces were there, as they were in this case.

12. The ten dollar bill, which was counterfeit and a bad one at that. It showed a portrait of Andrew Jackson instead of that of Alexander Hamilton.

    The secret service, following up on the counterfeit trail, discovered that a demented counterfeiter with a fixation on Jackson had engraved the bills. They were almost perfect otherwise. The moral is, know your presidents.

Solution to *Wedding Day* (p. 48)

Turn the clock around and get dressed. Somebody had turned it over to rest on its right side, and the correct time is about 9:05 A.M. This is clear because the cord, which is plugged in, emerges from the left-hand top. Cords always come from the bottom or lower portion of electric clocks—and for that matter, perhaps of all appliances.

In point of fact young Lochinvar not only got to the church on time, but he was ten minutes early, while Griselda got caught in a traffic jam and arrived fifteen minutes late. He forgave her readily, and they lived happily ever after.

LAWRENCE TREAT

Lawrence Treat, the author of over seventeen mystery books and countless short stories, is past president and now a director of Mystery Writers of America. He received an Edgar Award for Best Short Mystery of the Year in 1965, and a Special Edgar in 1978 for editing the *Mystery Writer's Handbook*. He lives on Martha's Vineyard.

By Lawrence Treat:

CRIME AND PUZZLEMENT: *24 Solve-Them-Yourself Picture Mysteries*
illustrated by Leslie Cabarga, $8.95

CRIME AND PUZZLEMENT 2: *24 More Solve-Them-Yourself Picture Mysteries*
illustrated by Kathleen Borowik, $8.95

CRIME AND PUZZLEMENT 3: *24 Solve-Them-Yourself Picture Mysteries*
illustrated by Paul Karasik, $8.95

YOU'RE THE DETECTIVE!: *24 Solve-Them-Yourself Picture Mysteries*
for the younger reader, illustrated by Kathleen Borowik, $8.95

Also Available:

TROUBLE IN BUGLAND: *A Collection of Inspector Mantis Mysteries*
by William Kotzwinkle, illustrated by Joe Servello, $14.95